Lila
and the
Crow

GABRIELLE GRIMARD

annick press
toronto + berkeley

Lila has just moved to a new city.
Every day she goes outside, sits on the sidewalk,
and scratches at the dirt with her stick.
A crow calls from across the road.

She traps bugs in a jar, then lets them go.
She plays hopscotch on the empty road.

Lila wishes she

had a friend.

But this morning she gets up early, dresses, and leaves the house.
With the wind in her hair and a smile on her face, she seems
to be flying on her way to school.

Her heart as light as a feather,
she imagines herself surrounded
by new friends.

The teacher, Mr. Nicholas, introduces Lila. She sees her classmates looking at her and can't wait to get to know them. Squirming at her desk, Lila taps her foot impatiently. Finally it's recess, and the children head out to play. Now is Lila's chance to make a friend!

But suddenly a voice rises above the others.
Nathan, the leader of the pack, shouts: *"A crow!*

A crow!

The new girl's hair

is dark like a crow!!"

The others stare at Lila. Some whisper to their friends, then turn away.

Lila
stands
alone,
holding
her ball.

On the way home, Lila's heart is as heavy as a stone.
A crow perches on the branch of an old oak tree,
its feathers as black as Lila's hair.

It caws and croaks as if it wants to tell
her something, but Lila just walks by.

The next day, Lila wears a knitted cap to hide her hair.

But as soon as Nathan sees her he cries out:

"A crow!

A crow!

The new girl's skin

is dark like a crow!!"

The others giggle and point. Lila's heart grows as heavy as two stones. She drops her head and slowly walks away.

As Lila heads home
after a long, lonely day,
the crow watches.

Lila looks up, but keeps walking. The crow spreads its wings and glides along behind her. Lila spins around. "Leave me alone!" she yells.

She doesn't want company,
not even a bird.

The third day, Lila goes to school wearing her cap and a sweater with a very, very high neck that she pulls up over her chin. Nathan peers at her for a moment. Then he shouts:

"A crow!

A crow!

The new girl's eyes are dark like a crow!!"

A few others laugh, quietly at first. Then more children join in and the laughter gets louder. Lila's heart grows as heavy as three stones. She sits at the edge of the playground until recess ends.

After school, Lila
kicks at everything
in sight: dead
leaves, branches,
and stones lying
on the ground.

The crow is watching her again. This time
it lands on the path and hops toward her.
Lila picks up a stone. As she hurls it at the
bird, it flies away.

Every day now, Lila hides—
under her cap, inside her sweater,
behind dark glasses.

She plays alone at recess and sits
by herself at lunch. After school,
she runs home as quickly as she can.

Weeks go by. The great autumn festival will soon
be here. The children chatter excitedly about the
costumes they're going to wear. All except Lila,
who dreams of having an invisibility cloak so
she can disappear forever.

It's the day before the great festival.
The classroom is decorated and the
children can't wait to show off their
costumes. Lila feels lonelier than ever.
Her heart is as heavy as a mountain
of stones.

Running home from school
as fast as she can, Lila trips.
As she crashes to the ground,
her heavy heart crumbles.

The crow lands near her.

Between her sobs, Lila lifts her head and for the first time really looks at the bird. She's surprised to see how beautiful its black feathers are, highlighted with purple. There's softness in the eyes of the creature watching her, and Lila has the strange feeling they have known each other for a long time. She takes a deep, shaky breath and wipes away her tears.

The crow comes closer to Lila
and seems to whisper in her ear.
Her heart lightens. She gets up,
and hopping on one foot and then
the other, follows the bird, which
flutters ahead of her into the woods.
The bird stops in a clearing. There,
under the canopy of trees, hundreds
of crows spread their great wings.
They circle the girl's body as she
stands in wonder.

When at last they fly away,
a shower of black feathers
settles at her feet.

Lila has an idea. She gathers a mountain
of feathers, stuffs them in her backpack,
and hurries home.

When the sun rises Lila is ready.
A flock of colorful little creatures heads
toward the school. Then Lila makes
her entrance, dark and majestic.

She is magnificent!

"A crow!

A crow!

Lila is a crow!!"

the children exclaim. Only Nathan is
speechless. The children crowd around
Lila, touching her soft feathers.

At that moment, her heart soars.

Lila is still called Crow. But she doesn't mind.

Now there is
something
different about
Mr. Nicholas's
class…

English translation by Paula Ayer
Edited by Debbie Rogosin
Designed by Natalie Olsen/Kisscut Design
First paperback printing March 2018
Annick Press Ltd.

We acknowledge the support of the Canada Council
for the Arts, the Ontario Arts Council, and the
participation of the Government of Canada/la
participation du gouvernement du Canada for our
publishing activities.

ONTARIO ARTS COUNCIL
CONSEIL DES ARTS DE L'ONTARIO
an Ontario government agency
un organisme du gouvernement de l'Ontario

Funded by the
Government
of Canada

Financé par le
gouvernement
du Canada

Canadä

For Gilles Tibo, my kind mentor,
for Colleen, who believed I could
write, for Paula, Ève, and the
crows of Yellowknife.

Cataloging in Publication

Grimard, Gabrielle, 1975–, author
Lila and the crow / Gabrielle Grimard.

Written by the author in French but not published.
Translated by Paula Ayer. First published in English.
Issued in print and electronic formats.
ISBN 978-1-55451-858-6 (hardback).
ISBN 978-1-55451-857-9 (paperback).
ISBN 978-1-55451-859-3 (html).
ISBN 978-1-55451-860-9 (pdf)

I. Title.

PS8613.R625L55 2016   JC813'.6   C2016-900587-9

Distributed in Canada by University of Toronto Press.
Published in the U.S.A. by Annick Press (U.S.) Ltd.
Distributed in the U.S.A. by Publishers Group West.

Printed in China

Visit us at: annickpress.com
Visit Gabrielle Grimard at: gabriellegrimard.com

Also available in e-book format. Please visit
annickpress.com/ebooks.html for more details.